DANIEL AND THE JUMBIES

by

Jules

April 2014

Dear Chloe—

Happy Spring!
May you always enjoy
the magic of reading.
Hope that you are having a
beautiful day!
Love Julia
"Jules"
XOXOXO

P.S. Thank you for
sharing your sunshine with
the world!
You
are
beaming!

Copyright © 2012 Julia Coffey Santella (Jules)

Palm Tree Peace Press
Ponte Vedra Beach, Florida, USA

In Loving Memory of Shelby, My Dear Daddy Bear.

ISBN: 0-9847-9600-2
ISBN-13: 978-0-9847960-0-7

DEDICATION

This book would not be possible without the incredible support and love of my extraordinary family, Kevin and Dylan. Thank you both for lighting up my every day, and for showing me the wonder of the Jumbies, in addition to all of the special magical adventures in this big, beautiful world. I love and cherish you both with all that I am…

CONTENTS

ACKNOWLEDGMENTS

To my family and friends, including those who have so marvelously become my chosen family. I adore each and every one of you, and will always be eternally grateful for your love and support. I hope that you know how truly special you are. You make the world a better place.

To my darling husband Kevin, many thanks for your tender guidance in bringing this story to fruition, and for patiently, lovingly, being there through it all.

To my favorite graphic designers, who happen to be my son and mother-thanks for all of your help with this project and with everything. Dylan, I am indebted to you for your cover creation and for putting your heart and soul into all that you do. You are the greatest son a mother could ever ask for.

To my dear editor Barbara Applin, across the pond-thank you for sticking with the Jumbies and this story, and for all of your hard work and loving effort to help share it with these special readers. I promise to convert this back to your beautiful English format as soon as I can (and any mistakes seen here are my own!). May your garden continue to prosper and flourish, and may you always do the same. I am forever grateful.

Special thanks to the stellar design team at CreateSpace for assembling this book into a pretty little package and for sharing so much of your precious time and tremendous expertise to bring it all together so flawlessly.

To my exceptional readers-thank you all for giving Daniel and the Jumbies a chance to come alive! I hope that you enjoy their story and take the magic with you wherever you may be. Please remember that every story has a bright side, just as every instance in life does. May you all experience the bright side of life with every precious day. Sending peace, laughter, and love to you all...

1

HOME SWEET HOME, CONNECTICUT!

Daniel was completely shocked when his parents told him something that would change his life forever. *Moving? To the Caribbean? This cannot be happening!* Daniel thought. Although he had no idea where the Caribbean was, he knew that he did not want to go. After living in a small town in Connecticut his whole life, this news was just too much to absorb. Apparently, Daniel's father, Ben, received a job offer that he couldn't refuse. It meant that he would have to uproot his family from the place that they so comfortably liked to call home.

The same news that made Daniel's father so happy created opposite feelings for Daniel. He had made some really good friends in the years that he had been attending Salisbury School. His best friend, James, was definitely not going to like this news at all. As soon as Daniel heard the announcement, the tall, blue-eyed, sometimes-stubborn boy left his parents at the kitchen table. He tore up the stairs, two at a time, until he was safely in his bedroom where he took a nosedive onto his pillow. *How could they do this to me?*

His parents knew that Daniel usually liked to be left alone when he was upset. Nevertheless, his mother, Nancy, heard his crying and crept through the partially opened door, into the galaxy that Daniel called his bedroom.

With the sun having just set, the stars and planets on Daniel's ceiling were starting to glow, and since Daniel did not feel like turning on the light, the only way for his mom to see where he lay crying was the moon and star-shaped nightlight.

"Daniel, sweetie, I know how you are feeling right now, but I would like to explain our reason for making this decision," his mom gently said, as she sat on the edge of the bed, and tried to smooth the blonde hair out of Daniel's eyes.

"How can you possibly know how I am feeling?" shouted Daniel, his voice still full of tears and anger.

"Because when your father first told me about this opportunity, the first thing I thought of was how much I am going to miss my friends and your grandmother, but now that I know more about it, I realize that it will be a good move for our family."

"Why does it have to be now, Mom, can't it wait until I have to go to high school?" he asked hopefully, starting to settle down a bit.

"No, sweetie, but you will be able to finish out the year at Salisbury since there are only two months left," Daniel's mom said tenderly, "and you will have plenty of time to spend with your friends. Besides, we will be back to visit as much as we can."

"Where is the Caribbean? What is this job? Do I have to go to school there? Where will we…?" and he got cut off.

"Daniel, I know that you have a lot of questions, and your father and I will answer them all for you, but right now it is getting late and you have school tomorrow. I don't want you to worry about this, because the important thing is that we will be together as a family, and we will actually get to see your father more than we do now." Daniel's mom took a deep breath, and then continued, "Many people consider the island where we are moving a paradise, so I am sure it is just beautiful. Try to get some sleep, and we'll talk about this tomorrow. You know that we love you very much."

"Yes, we do, son," Daniel's father was in the doorway, listening to his wife, "and I promise you that this move will be an exciting adventure. You'll love it. Now please try to get some sleep."

After they left his room, Daniel stared up at the ceiling, not believing that this news could possibly be a good thing. He decided to tell his best friend, James, tomorrow at recess and see what he had to say about it. In the meantime, after tossing and turning for what seemed like hours, he finally drifted off to sleep.

2

MOVING ON

The next morning, Daniel awoke to the aroma of bacon and coffee, and as he opened his eyes, the reality of the night before began to kick in. He was moving. Away from his friends, his school, his room, and everything that he knew and loved. This was just not fair, but as his father always reminded him, "Life isn't fair".

Despite the usual early morning rush of everyone getting ready at once, the three Hawthornes were able to sit down to breakfast and discuss more about their new plans. For the most part, Daniel stayed quiet and listened.

"I will have to get a head start on setting up the business, so I will be flying down there at the end of this month," Daniel's father said to no one in particular, hoping they were both listening. "You both will have plenty to do with all of the packing and getting rid of the 'non-necessities'. Since I have already found us a nice place, the transition should be easy."

Easy? Daniel knew what a transition was, and he did not think that it was going to be easy.

His father continued. "Hurricane season starts in the middle of August, so I want to make sure we are completely settled in and are prepared for anything. My buddy Jonathon said it's best to stock up on goods and make sure all of the hurricane shutters are secure far in advance."

"At least we don't have to worry about that for a little while," Daniel's mom chimed in. "Right now I want to tell Daniel a little bit about where we are moving to, so he feels more comfortable about it."

"I'm late for the bus," Daniel said quickly, standing up and grabbing his backpack and lunch that was packed lovingly by his mom. Before his parents could stop him, he was out of the door and on his way to the bus stop, trying not to think of strange places and hurricanes and leaving his friends.

The morning at school went slowly, especially since Daniel could not wait to tell his best friend about what was happening to him. At recess, Daniel and James went to their favorite spot under a sycamore tree, perched themselves on the overgrown roots, and began their usual game of Spy. They kept a notebook and observed other kids on the playground and took notes as to their actions, hoping to solve crimes like finding missing stolen locker supplies or figuring out who had vandalized the outside wall of the gym. Today, Daniel was in no mood to play Spy, and decided to just blurt out what was on his mind. "I'm moving far away."

James did not realize at first what he was talking about. "On the playground? What do you mean, you are moving far away? You're sitting right in front of me!"

"No, James, my family has to move because my dad got this silly job that he calls 'a good opportunity' and we are leaving right after school ends!"

"That's okay, I'll just ride my bike over to your new place, and we can still hang out," James, always the positive one, decided aloud.

"You don't understand. We are going to an island that is very far away. You have to take a plane to get there and I don't even know where it is."

"I'll come visit. If it is an island, it must have water around it, and we can do some cool things like swim and fish and explore. Besides, it's a long time away. We can have fun before you go, we have plenty of time," James said.

And that was that. The two best friends went back to their game of Spy, and before they knew it, they had forgotten all about the big move. Kind of.

3

BRIEF GOODBYES

The "plenty of time" that James talked about ended up going by very quickly. While Daniel finished his school year, his mom and grandmother packed up all of their things. They decided to get rid of the heavy sweaters and other belongings around the house that one simply does not need on a tropical island. As moving time got closer, Daniel began to daydream about what it might actually be like in his new home. *Will there be anyone my age there? Of course,* he thought, *there are kids my age everywhere, but none that will be like James.*

Moving Day had officially arrived, and James was at the Hawthornes' house to say goodbye to his best friend. As the movers put the last piece of furniture on the truck, Daniel turned to James and reminded him of his promise to visit.

"The name of the island that we are moving to is St. John, so don't forget that we are going to go fishing when you come to see me at my new place," Daniel said, his voice changing mid-sentence, as he fought back tears.

"I will be there, and you'll be fine," James said to Daniel. "Besides, we can still write and we have each other's email addresses, so it will seem like we still live right down the street from one another."

"You are right, James, and we'll always be best buds, right?"

"You got it, Daniel, now get a move on and let me know how the trip goes." James got on his bike. After slapping Daniel on the back and waving to Daniel's parents, he rode off down the street, knowing that it would be a long time before he would see his best friend again.

"We have a plane to catch, son," Daniel's dad called out to him, mostly to distract him from missing his best friend already, "and you still have a lot to do to help us clean this place up..."

The last thing Daniel felt like doing was cleaning, but he knew that it was inevitable, so he followed his parents through the only home he had ever known, and while he helped do a final check, he silently said goodbye to all of the rooms, one by one.

And then, after many hugs and tears, the three Hawthornes said a long farewell to Grandma, who was already planning her first visit to St. John. The rest of the family was hoping that they could talk her into eventually joining them. But for now, Grandma simply waved goodbye from the porch of the house (that now belonged to a stranger), as the airport taxi pulled away.

4

WRONG SIDE OF THE ROAD

My *parents were right*, thought Daniel; *this trip sure is an adventure.* To get to their new home, they had to take a plane to an island called St. Thomas, and upon landing, Daniel looked out at the palm trees and aqua sea, amazed by the beauty of it all. When the plane landed, the passengers got off by using stairs that took them right outside, into the balmy tropical breezes. After collecting their bags, the Hawthornes took a taxi, (which to Daniel looked just like a van), to the ferry station. As the taxi sped around the winding roads, Daniel noticed something very odd. The driver was on the wrong side of the road! Actually, everyone was driving on the left side of the road instead of the right!

Ben noticed that his son was apprehensive. "In the Virgin Islands, everyone drives on the left side of the road. The islands were founded by the Danish and the residents decided to keep this tradition and make it a law, and it just stuck. You will get used to it. When I first came back to Connecticut after coming here, I thought it was strange to see people driving on the right!"

Daniel continued to stare out at the activities going on in a place where nothing was familiar. He observed many people working, and others bustling around in outdoor shopping areas that looked like flea markets. He also saw many bright colored houses, some large and some that were unfinished. He was so intrigued by the differences he saw compared to his life in Connecticut, that he did not realize that they had reached their destination. Well, not the final destination. There was one more leg of their journey left; they still needed to board the ferry that would take them to St. John.

A very nice West Indian man came to collect their luggage, which got placed on the ferry before the people were allowed to board. The Hawthornes stood outside, waiting to be told that they could join their luggage on the commuter boat, as Daniel looked down at the school of minnows that were swimming right next to the dock. *So far, this trip is not so bad after all.*

The twelve-minute ride on the ferry proved to be even more beautiful than his father had described. Daniel started to relax and did not feel as worried about what lay ahead, and he enjoyed looking out onto the unknown islands, wondering what it would be like to live here all of the time. He felt the ferry begin to slow down, and he turned to see the island of St. John, his new home.

"We're coming into Cruz Bay," his father explained, as someone waved up at them from the dock. It was Ben's partner, Jonathon, who owned the charter company that flew amphibians in the islands. With him was his daughter, Paige, whom Daniel had never met.

They departed from the ferry quickly and Daniel and his mom were being introduced to Paige, who had grown up on St. John and knew no other home. Jonathon helped them with their bags and led them to his Jeep, which had the company logo, "Seaplane Charters", written on the side in colorful lettering, along with a picture of one of their planes.

Paige seems pretty nice, thought Daniel, *for a girl*, and he noticed the contrast of her tan skin with her long braided blonde hair as she excitedly told the Hawthornes about the island, while pointing out of the Jeep window. "...and this is where the governor lives, right next to the National Park office. More than two-thirds of this island has been National Park since Laurence Rockefeller bought it in the 1950s, with the condition that it would remain untouched. So no one can build on it, they can just enjoy it and help preserve its beauty."

"You sure seem to know a lot about the island, Paige," Nancy commented.

"Living here my whole life helped teach me a lot, and even though I have visited the States a couple of times, St. John is home and I find its history interesting," Paige replied, and then she turned toward Daniel. She bombarded him with questions. "So what do you like to do? Do you play sports? Do you like school?"

"I like to ride my bike," Daniel said shyly, "and sometimes kick a ball around with my friend James. School's okay," then he chuckled a little. "How about you?"

"I am involved in the St. John community a lot. I like to help other people. We don't have as many sports here as you probably do, but we have fun," Paige explained, wanting to show her new friends how nice the island was. Then she added, "And I love school."

After about twenty minutes of more windy roads, some St. John history, and a very steep driveway, Jonathon finally pulled up to the Hawthornes' new home. As they got out of the Jeep, Daniel was tired, but wanted to take it all in, because everything was so new to him. He followed the group down the path to the front door, anxious to see his new room.

5

WHAT A VIEW

Their new house was partially furnished, since they could not bring all of their furniture to such a warm and moist climate. Daniel went from room to room, looking at the unfamiliar bamboo couches and chairs, and enjoying the bright walls, decorated in what he soon would refer to as Caribbean colors. As he came back to the main living area, he was slightly upset to realize that he hadn't seen his new room.

"Where is my room?" he asked his parents, hoping that he would not be sharing a bedroom with them.

"See that ladder?" Ben asked his son, "Once you get to the top, everything you see is all yours."

Daniel could not climb the ladder fast enough. When he got to the top, he could not believe what he saw. It was the biggest bedroom he had ever seen, and it was all his! Not only that, once he got off of the ladder and walked around, he also saw his very own bathroom. In his new bedroom, there was a bamboo desk, where someone had put a gift bag with Daniel's name on it.

"Open it," his mother said, as she climbed the ladder, slightly slower than her son and requiring a bit more effort.

Daniel ripped open his gift, thinking that this was better than Christmas, as he saw two boxes of glow-in-the-dark stars and planets. "For my new room?" he asked.

"You can put them up yourself, unless you want help," his mom said, nodding a big "yes" and smiling brightly.

"Thank you!" Daniel excitedly replied, already planning his strategic placement of his new galaxy. He barely noticed when Jonathon and Paige yelled their goodbyes up to the loft. All he could think of was how much he wished James could see his new room.

It only got better when Daniel finally came down the ladder to explore the outside of their new home. Standing on the deck, he looked out onto the most amazing view he could ever have imagined.

"There is Tortola, one of the British Virgin Islands." His father appeared, pointing to various spots and explaining them to Daniel. "And there is Jost Van Dyke, Norman Island, and Cooper Island." He proudly continued, pointing down directly in front of them. "And right here is where we are going to put the swimming pool right after hurricane season."

"Swimming pool? Wow!" Daniel was so excited that he hardly heard the part about hurricane season. This was just too much for one day. *Wait until I email James*, he thought, *he will never believe any of this.*

It was time to pick up some groceries since it was getting late, and even though Daniel thought he was old enough to stay at home alone, he decided to go with his parents so he could see more of the island.

6

GROCERY SHOPPING ON ISLAND TIME

The grocery store trip was another learning adventure. As Ben drove, he pointed out different points of interest to his wife and son, such as sugar mill ruins that had been there for many years. Daniel allowed himself to drift into a dream-like state, partly because he was slightly tired from the plane ride.

As he looked out of the window into his new world, he took everything in as he thought of what his new life would be like. So far, he was happy about where they were living; especially his room, but he still missed James and his grandmother a lot.

The grocery store was quite different from the supermarkets that Daniel was used to. It was much smaller, with not as many items to choose from. This was okay with Daniel, because it would mean less time in one of his not-so-favorite places. While his mother was inspecting avocadoes, he glanced down the aisle and noticed a West Indian boy who appeared to be about his age. Daniel saw him look back at him, outwardly curious about the new kid in town. It seemed to Daniel that the boy must live around here, since it looked as if he was comfortable in his surroundings. He assumed that the tall and thin lady with the boy must be the boy's mother.

Just as Daniel was contemplating the thought of a potential new friend, the mysterious child disappeared behind the lady that he was with, and Daniel did not spot him again before they left the store.

After helping his parents unload all of the groceries, Daniel went up to his room and wanted to put his new glow-in-the-dark stars on the ceiling. He barely got up the ladder and across the room before he realized that he was completely exhausted. So, he lay down as he listened to all of the unfamiliar noises outside. Soon he drifted off to sleep, dreaming of stars and moons and planets that were very far away.

7

A TOUR OF PARADISE

ensing the ceiling fan whirling above his head, Daniel slowly opened his eyes on the first morning in his new home, and took awhile to realize where he was. He turned on his side and as his eyes came into focus, he noticed a gecko speeding past him, running up the wall. "Cool," he said to himself, as he got out of bed and proceeded to place the glow-in-the-dark stars on the wall. After hearing some activity downstairs, Daniel quickly got dressed and shinnied down his ladder.

His mother and father were both sitting at the kitchen table, coffee in hand and talking excitedly about their plans for the day. His Dad was going to take Daniel and his Mom on a real tour of the island, including his father's favorite beach. So, after eating quickly and telling his parents about the gecko he had seen in his room, they were applying their bug spray and sunscreen and piling into the Jeep.

"You will be seeing a lot of those geckos, Daniel, so I am glad that you like them. They are good for us since they like to eat bugs," Ben explained.

"Do they always move that fast?" Daniel asked.

"Yes, most of the time, because they are afraid of us, and because they have to be fast to catch the bugs." Ben continued with a slight warning for Daniel, "Don't bother trying to grab them by their tails, because they can shed their tails if they are caught. It's not a pleasant sight, believe me."

Wow, thought Daniel, *this place sure is different.* Then he replied to his Dad, "That is cool."

His parents looked at each other and smiled.

Taking the many curves and turns like a pro, Ben drove around the island, which was only nine miles across, but took a long time since the speed limit was only 25 miles per hour. He showed his family the east end of the island, which not too many people lived on, as it was quite a distance from "town". He also drove them by Coral Bay, where they stopped for a cheeseburger at Skinny Legs, the local place for good hamburgers as well as good company. Daniel thought a lot of people there looked like real pirates!

Ben ran into a few people he had met before and proudly introduced them to his wife and son. There was much laughter and many nice people, although Daniel did not see anyone who was even close to his age.

The next stop was the one that Daniel was the most excited about. The beach! He was thinking that there would be a bunch of parking spaces like at home, but when they got there, his dad had to maneuver the Jeep awkwardly into a hidden parking spot amongst the trees. As they got out of the Jeep, Daniel noticed a brown road sign with white letters that said "Jumbie Beach".

"Well, where is it, Dad?" he asked, looking around and only seeing wooden stairs but no sand or water.

"Let's go and I'll show you, and be careful not to step on any geckos or mongooses on your way down," Ben said while smiling.

"Mongooses?" Daniel asked.

Nancy cut in. "About one hundred years ago, the people of this island brought them in to get rid of the rat problem. The funny thing is, rats only come out at night so the plan didn't work too well. They look kind of like ferrets. Remember when you wanted a ferret as a pet?"

Daniel laughed and said, "Yeah, of course I remember, because you didn't let me...I, uh, still don't see a beach."

"You'll see," Ben replied.

So down the rickety wooden stairs they climbed, carrying all of their beach supplies, until Daniel could finally see beyond the swaying palm trees, that this was, in fact, a beach. And it was not like any of the beaches that he was used to. This beach was laden with clean, white sand and crystal clear light blue water. The first thing that Daniel did when they arrived was throw down his towel and sunscreen, and run as fast as he could into the glorious sea.

8

A NEW FRIEND ON JUMBIE BEACH

The water was much warmer than Daniel expected, and felt so good on his muscles and skin. For a long moment, he forgot all about his friends at home, his old room, and his fear about moving to this foreign place.

After swimming and playing with fish for almost an hour, Daniel finally got out of the water. He noticed that since they had arrived, more people had occupied the beach, but not too many. As he glanced at his new surroundings, Daniel recognized the boy from the market, who was there with his mother.

"Why don't you go and introduce yourself?" Daniel's Dad asked him, noticing his curiosity.

"Because, Dad, you just don't go up to a stranger and start talking to him."

"Here, you do," his father said, "St. John is a very friendly place, and since there are only about five thousand people on the whole island, you get to know everyone in no time."

Five thousand people sounded like an awful lot to Daniel, but he decided it would not hurt to meet someone his own age, so he took his Dad's advice.

"Hi, I'm Daniel, and I–I– just moved here," he said slowly, sounding unsure of himself. "Do you live here?"

The young boy spoke first. "Yeah, I've always lived here."

"Welcome to Paradise," the boy's mother said to Daniel, while smiling. "This is my son, Noah, and my name is Miss Walter. It's nice to have you here."

"Thank you," Daniel replied, then turned to Noah and asked, "Do you wanna swim?"

"Sure, but let me show you a cool place first," Noah responded, then turned on his bare feet and dashed across the sand.

Daniel was right behind him. "Where are we going?"

"Not far, this beach is small but there is a lot to see. Why did you move here?" Noah asked, as he headed toward the palms.

"My Dad is a pilot and started an amphibian business. An amphibian is a plane that can take off and land in the water…"

"I know what an amphibian is, silly. I see them all of the time."

"Oh," Daniel put his head down. He had a lot to learn about this unusual new place.

They reached a private little spot behind some huge boulders. The ground was lined with smooth leaves and the area was surrounded by conch shells that Daniel had never seen, except in books.

"What is this place?" Daniel asked his new friend, as he thought of James.

"It is my secret fort," Noah explained, "I go here when I want to hide, or just hang out by myself."

Daniel looked toward the sea, and realized that he could still see his parents, as well as the bright Caribbean sun reflecting off of the clear water.

"This fort is great," Daniel said, "what made you bring me here?"

"I knew that you would keep it quiet. I saw you in the market yesterday. Did you just get here?"

"Yeah," Daniel answered, "I guess I still have a lot to get used to."

"I'll show you around," Noah said, as he poked at a gecko with a long stick. "Do you know why they call this 'Jumbie Beach'?"

"No, what is a 'Jumbie'?"

"You do have a lot to learn. A Jumbie is a spirit that can be very good or very bad. Only the really old and the really young can see a Jumbie."

"Are they scary?"

"Oh, yes, I saw one once."

"What did it look like?" Daniel's eyes opened wide, as he listened for Noah's answer.

"When I saw the Jumbie, I was in my bed one night, about to go to sleep. All of a sudden, my whole body started sweating, and I felt the room get hotter and hotter. I felt like I could not catch my breath." Noah was shaking as he remembered, while he continued his story. "Then I heard a very weird noise, which sounded like a..."

"DANIELLLLL!" it was Ben Hawthorne's voice, shouting from the beach. "DANIEL, where are you? We have to go!"

"Just when it was getting good," Daniel said to Noah. Then he turned toward the water, and the sound of his father's voice. "I'm coming, Dad!" he yelled.

"I'll tell you the rest later. Where do you live?" Noah asked.

"In Coral Bay."

"Me, too," Noah said in an excited voice. "Maybe I will see you there."

"Yeah. I better go." Daniel said quickly, not wanting to get in trouble for sneaking off.

"Make sure you go back a different way. I don't want any adults to find this place. Do you want to meet me back here tomorrow, around the same time?"

"I'll try," Daniel happily replied. "I have to see what we are doing. See ya later."

"Yeah, see ya."

Daniel crept back through the brush, wondering why his parents were in such a hurry, as he listened to the unknown animals scurrying at his feet.

9

BACK TO THE FORT

That evening, Daniel decided to email James.

Hey James,

You wouldn't believe this place! There are palm trees everywhere, and the water is see-through! You can see your feet while you are standing in the sea if you look down. I even spotted a sea turtle when I was swimming! And there is this boy named Noah who grew up here that showed me a secret hiding place and he told me about these spirits called Jumbies that haunt people. I wish you could visit right now! Write soon.

Daniel

P.S. My father said we are putting in a pool too.

He won't believe me about the water, Daniel thought. *Wait until he sees this place. It is not as bad as I imagined.* As Daniel laid his head on the pillow, he drifted off to sleep and dreamt of ghosts and fish and geckos.

The next morning Daniel woke up early. He heard strange noises outside, and looked out of the window. He could not believe his eyes when he saw three Billy Goats gnawing on some weeds, right outside his window! After he caught sight of the rocks that they were knocking over with their munching, Daniel realized what had been making all the racket. The goats were causing an avalanche of rolling rocks, all the way down to the side of the house. Daniel was not sure it was a good thing, so he shouted out the window for them to scram.

After breakfast, Daniel asked, "Can we please go back to Jumbie Beach, Dad?"

"I don't know, we have a lot to do today, and we also have to register you in your new school," his father answered.

"Already?" Daniel made his face all squishy.

"Yes, learning is another one of those things in life that is unavoidable," his mom chimed in.

"Okay, but if we have time I hope we can stop by Jumbie. Even if it is really quick."

"We'll see," both of Daniel's parents said at the same time. They all laughed.

"Dad, you never got to tell me why they call it 'Jumbie Beach'", Daniel remembered aloud.

"I'm sure you'll hear a lot about Jumbies the longer we live here," Ben said to his son. "They are spirits that some people believe are bad."

"Does anyone think they are good?"

"Well I think people hope that Jumbies can be good. That is why they do things like name a beach after them; they want to make the spirits happy." Ben glanced out the window for a moment in deep thought, then continued. "I also heard that Jumbies have magical, uh, healing powers, or at least that is what some people believe."

"What do you believe, Dad?" asked Daniel slowly.

"All I know is when I ask people around here about Jumbies, they tend to change the subject. Now let's get going because we have a lot to get done today."

Daniel made a mental note to talk more about this with his new friend Noah.

The day was filled with more errands. Daniel met so many new people; he could hardly remember any of their names. They stopped by the hardware store, the post office, the clothing store to pick up a new bathing suit, and even went to the Juice Shack to try a banana smoothie. Daniel could barely absorb it all; everything was so unfamiliar to him. People seemed to have a different accent than he was used to, sort of like the one that Noah had. Then he remembered that he was supposed to meet Noah that afternoon. Just as he was about to ask his parents, his father said, "We have just a minute to stop by Jumbie Beach as promised. You can jump in the water but then we have to go."

"Thanks, Dad," Daniel said, barely containing his excitement. This time, Jumbie Beach was not as "crowded", if you could call it that, as the day before. Daniel saw no sign of Noah, but when he was looking around, Jonathon's daughter Paige was walking up to him.

"Hi Daniel, how's it going?" she asked him.

"Good, I guess," Daniel said with his hands in his pockets, as he pushed the sand back and forth beneath his feet. "This place isn't so bad."

"Well, let me know if you need anything. I'll see you in school," and off Paige skipped into the water before Daniel could reply.

"I'll be right back, Mom and Dad, I just need to check on something," Daniel said to his parents, then headed toward the secret hiding place.

When he saw the top of a head with black curly hair, Daniel knew that he was not too late. Noah was sitting in his usual spot, carving something that looked like a fish out of a piece of wood.

"Hey Daniel," Noah said, "thought you weren't coming."

"I couldn't wait to hear the rest of the story about the Jumbies," Daniel said, then looking back down at the woodcarving, asked, "Whatcha doing?"

"Oh, just making another fish. I learned to carve wood from Downtown Leon, and I've been trying to make a bunch of different fish."

"Downtown who?"

"Oh", Noah replied, while giggling. "Everyone here has a nickname, especially if they're known for something. Downtown Leon is always seen in the same spot downtown, so someone started calling him that, and the name just stuck."

"What is your nickname?"

"I think I'm too young for a nickname. But soon you'll meet Dozer Tom, Barnacle Bob, and Sailor Sam and maybe even Parrot Dave. He carries a parrot on his shoulder no matter where he's going."

"Wow, the longer I'm here, the more I realize how different everything is from home."

"Different in a good way or bad?" Noah asked.

Daniel had to think about that one for a moment. "Good, I think."

"That's a positive sign. Now where did I leave off about the Jumbies?"

"You were saying that it got really hot in your bedroom and you were short of breath. You never got to tell me about the sound that you heard."

"Oh, yeah. I was talking about my mother, who was shouting through the door and asking me if I was all right. You see, she cannot see the Jumbie but I must've been screaming or something because she came running. When she got inside my room, there was no more sign of the Jumbie." Noah's brow was sweating, but not necessarily from the humid weather.

"So, what did it look like?" Daniel curiously asked.

"Funny you should ask that question, since different people have seen different things. As much as I try to block it out, I will never forget what I saw that night." Noah looked down at the wood scrapings, and dug out another piece before continuing. "I remember seeing something that looked like a giant ball of fire, but it was shaped like a person, sort of. And its eyes were bulging circles, a color I had never seen, sort of blackish…"

"Daniel, where did you go this time?" His mother shouted from a few hundred feet away.

"Coming, Ma!" he yelled, not believing his rotten luck. *Would I ever get to hear Noah's story?* Turning to his friend, Daniel quickly said, "I'll talk to you soon, Noah. Maybe I'll see ya in school next week. I gotta go."

10

FIRST DAY OF SCHOOL

They got to the Coral Bay School just in time. Daniel was the last student who needed to be signed up for classes, and he just made it. As his parents filled out all of the necessary paperwork, Daniel decided to roam the area to get acquainted with his new surroundings. *Not very big,* he thought, *I wonder how many kids go here.* He went outside and did not think the playground setup was too shabby, but as he headed toward the classrooms, Daniel thought there was something very important missing. *The sycamore tree, of course!* Where was there room to sneak off into a corner and play Spy, and who was going to play it with him? *That is really what is missing,* thought Daniel; *it's James.* He suddenly did not feel like taking the tour of the school after all.

Daniel sat on the bench outside and waited for his parents, as he continued to think of everything he missed about home. Mostly James and Grandma, but it was more than that. It was the comfort of knowing every nook and cranny of his town, and his house, and all of the other great things about home, which he would never get to see again. He looked up to see a donkey crossing the road and thought about how odd it was in this new place. At least in Connecticut there were "normal" animals! After feeling sorry for himself for what seemed like an hour, Daniel finally saw his parents coming out of the school.

"We're all set," Ben Hawthorne said with a big grin, "let's go home."

Daniel kept his eyes on the ground. "Yeah, home. Whatever."

Looking at each other, Daniel's parents decided to remain quiet about this latest mood. They knew that the adjustment was going to take a long time, and they had discussed privately how well they thought Daniel had been taking it all, so far.

That night, Daniel went up to his room right after dinner. He was so beat from the day's events that it was not long before he fell into a fitful sleep. This time, his dreams were filled with visions of fear; there were huge hands coming at him, trying to grab his throat. Daniel could barely catch his breath. It was not until he sat up in bed and noticed the cold sweat all over his body that he realized it was only a nightmare.

"Geez, I wonder if that was a Jumbie or just a terrible dream," Daniel said aloud. After that, it took him a very long time to drift back to sleep.

11

FUN RAISER

"Daniel, you won't believe it," his mother was still holding her coffee mug as she hung up the phone. "You will not be starting school next week like we thought."

"What are you talking about?" Daniel asked, rubbing his tired eyes.

"There is not enough money to run the air conditioners, and since it's so hot, the schools can't open until the money is raised."

"Raised?" Daniel was stunned, and secretly pleased that he had more vacation time than he thought. "Who's supposed to raise the money?"

"The citizens of Coral Bay, which obviously includes us." His mother continued. "Jonathon just told me that they are holding a pie-throwing contest at Pickle's Deli this weekend. I guess there are people who offer to get a pie thrown in their face, for a fee that is determined by the highest bidder."

"Cool!" Daniel did not notice his mother's perplexed take on the whole situation. "Can I throw one of the pies?"

"That depends on how much allowance money you have saved," his mom replied. "Let's talk to your father about this one. It is definitely for a good cause."

Ben Hawthorne walked in the door, hearing the last part of his wife's comment. "What cause are we discussing now?" he asked with a smile, while placing his keys on the counter.

"Oh, nothing much, just for Daniel's school to open for the year," Nancy said sarcastically.

"What on earth are you talking about?" Ben was confused.

Daniel wandered off as his mother explained the situation to his Dad. He decided to go exploring around the outside of the house, to see what other critters he could find. As he walked along the side of the house (where the Billy Goats played), Daniel glanced at the ground. He spotted an animal that seemed to be about the size of his palm. It had a huge decorative shell, and was cruising up the hill pretty fast. He recognized it from one of the books that his teacher used to read to his class. "A hermit crab," he said aloud, as he reached down to pick it up.

"OUCH!" Daniel screamed, quickly tossing the poor crab, which went hurling through the air toward places unknown. He must have forgotten that when hermit crabs detect harm, they reach around their shell and pinch the culprit. Daniel noticed some blood, so he thought it would be best to run inside and wash it off.

"...so we will all be going on Saturday to participate in the pie-throwing fun," his mother finished telling Ben. After seeing Daniel come in the door with his hand bleeding, Nancy Hawthorne ran over to see what had happened.

"It's just a little cut, Mom, that's all. Don't make such a big deal about it. I just got pinched by a hermit crab."

His mother helped Daniel clean up his cut, and then said, "Daniel, you have to be careful around here. You aren't familiar with the area yet and there is no telling what you might run into."

A *Jumbie*, thought Daniel, *is what I might run into.* Instead, he said to his mom, "I'm not a little kid anymore, Mom, and I know what I should and shouldn't touch."

"Okay, whatever you say. All that I am asking is that you are careful. Now let's eat some dinner. I thought we'd cook out tonight," Nancy said, heading toward the grill.

Daniel loved when they cooked out at home. *Wait a minute. This is my home now*, Daniel thought. This was going to take a lot of getting used to. He decided to run upstairs before dinner to see if James had written back.

He was excited at the thought of a message from James. As he booted up his computer, he thought about how much he missed him. Yes! James had written back, and Daniel got really close to the screen so he would not miss one word.

Daniel,

Hey! It was good to hear from you. It sounds like you have a lot going on there. You aren't missing much here. School started, and my class is okay. It's just not the same as when you were here. There is no one who knows how to play Spy like you do. I've been hanging out with your old pal Nick, and he's not bad, even though he likes to play sissy games a lot. I can't wait to hear more about Jumbies. Can I see one when I visit? Write soon.

James

P.S. How's school?

I can't believe James would hang out with someone like Nick, thought Daniel. Nick used to bother both of them almost every day in school. It would seem that Nick wanted to play, but he always went about it the wrong way. He was just mean. Obviously James was being sarcastic when he called Nick his "old pal". *If only I hadn't moved away,* thought Daniel, *then James would not be stuck being friends with Nick.*

Daniel wanted to write back to James right away. He sat still for a moment, thinking, and then began to write.

James,

I can't believe you are hanging out with Nick, of all people! Anyway, you won't believe this one. I don't have to start school for at least two weeks! It turns out that they don't have enough money to run the air conditioners. The town is having some crazy pie-throwing contest to raise the money. Can you believe it? I have to go eat dinner but I promise to write soon. There is nothing more to tell about the Jumbies, but I will let you know. Right now all I can say about them is that they are scary. See ya later.

Daniel

Daniel went to bed that night hoping that he would not dream of Jumbies, or any other "spirits" for that matter. He was tired enough to fall asleep as soon as he lay down. Luckily, that night in his dreams, he did not have any encounters with the Jumbies. Or, at least none that he remembered.

12

ONE, TWO, THREE, THROW!

On Saturday morning, Daniel awoke to one of the strangest sounds he had ever heard. It was as if there were nails hitting the roof above his head! It did not take him long to realize that it was pouring outside. It sounded like nails because the roof was made of aluminum, and the power of the rain was so strong that the noise was extremely loud.

"There is no way that they can have the pie-throwing contest now," Daniel said to his mother in the kitchen. He felt as if he was yelling to be heard over the pounding rain.

"Your father said that these rain storms don't last too long," Daniel's mother stated as she placed a bowl of cereal in front of her son. "It should be fine by this afternoon."

Daniel's mother was right. By the time they got to Pickle's Deli, the only sign of rain was a puddle or two in the dirt road. The sky had cleared up and the bright sun was beating down on the island. There was already a nice sized crowd gathering in front of the deli. As Daniel and Nancy were getting out of the car, Daniel's father Ben came walking toward them.

"We're all set here," Ben said. He was wearing jeans that were covered in mud. "We just got done setting up the tables where the pies are going. There's going to be both chocolate and strawberry pies to throw."

"I'm glad I am not the one doing all of the laundry," Daniel's mother said with a smile. "What can we do to help?"

"Well, we already have five volunteers to get pies thrown in their faces. Want to join them, Daniel?"

"No thanks, Dad, I'd rather be doing the throwing," Daniel replied. "Where can I sign up?"

Ben answered, "No need, son, just be right here when they start the bidding."

"Okay." Daniel sat on the steps and waited for the bidding to begin. Looking around, he noticed that this was not just any old deli. It was not even closed in like they were in Connecticut. The deli counter faced out onto a small open porch with picnic tables placed haphazardly around. There were a few shelves with canned goods for sale, and a restroom that looked like the outhouses Daniel had read about in his history books. There was also a section for the band to set up when they played there, and Daniel noticed some adults getting a microphone ready and talking amongst themselves. It was almost time for the bidding.

"Hi Daniel," Paige announced unexpectedly, "Are you going to be in the contest?"

"Oh, hi, Paige," Daniel said, "I was hoping that I would get to throw one of the pies. Do you know how much these things usually cost?"

"Well, last year they were trying to raise money for the tennis courts," Paige answered, "and some of the bids got up to one hundred dollars."

"One hundred dollars?" Daniel asked a bit loudly, while remaining completely shocked. Then, concealing his surprise, said to Paige, "That's no big deal."

"Okay, have fun. I'm going to get an ice cream cone. I will be watching you later. See ya." And, as quickly as she had arrived, Paige disappeared.

Daniel reached his hand into his pocket and pulled out its contents. He counted exactly thirty dollars. *Not bad, for only getting two dollars a week allowance,* he thought, *but not good enough.*

Noah could not have shown up at a better time. "Hey, Daniel, what's going on?" he asked as he glanced down at the wadded up money in Daniel's hand.

"Hey, Noah. I was just seeing how much money I have to bid, but I guess it's not enough," Daniel said in a disappointed tone.

"I have an idea," Noah said, pulling out a pouch that looked pretty full. "Let's pool our money together so we can have the highest bid."

"How much do you have?"

After counting the contents of his pouch, Noah happily said, "Oh, about sixty dollars."

"Wow, where did you get all of that?" Daniel's eyes got big.

"I know some people who live on my street that usually don't come to these events, so I knocked on some doors and asked if they would like to donate something for a good cause," Noah said proudly.

"That was nice of you," Daniel said, thinking that he had a lot to learn about his new friend.

"Well, actually, my mom made me do it," Noah admitted, "I wasn't in any rush to start school. So, do you want to do this together?"

"Yeah, but who will throw the pie?" Daniel asked, thinking that he would like to throw a gooey chocolate one.

"You can throw it," Noah said generously, "I got to do it last year. Look, they're starting."

The two new friends got closer to the stage and listened to the announcer start the bidding process. The first person to volunteer to get creamed with a pie was the owner of Pickle's Deli, whose name was Matilda Burns. Apparently, everyone wanted a chance to throw a pie at Matilda since the bidding got up to one hundred and twenty dollars! Daniel did not mind missing out on this one since it would give him a chance to see how it was done.

Matilda Burns was wearing a crisp white apron over a printed floral dress. The winner of the bidding was the man who owned the only other deli on the island. His deli was all the way in Cruz Bay, so there was not much competition between them. But, to Daniel, it looked as if they were competitive as the pie thrower wound up with a bright red strawberry pie, and whipped it right into Matilda Burns' face!

The red and white colored cream dripped down the front of her apron, as Matilda ran her hand through her strawberry-filled hair. Daniel thought she looked as though she was going to throw a fit. Just then, Matilda Burns cracked a huge smile and gave the pie thrower a giant hug. They both laughed as they looked down at themselves, even though they were coated with a big strawberry pie mess.

The rest of the event was just as much fun, especially when Daniel and Noah won the bid for the last volunteer. They did not recognize this very tall large man, who seemed to them to be about eighty years old. It did not matter if he knew who the man was. Daniel was still excited to be able to throw the pie.

"Chocolate, please," Daniel told the lady behind the counter, who quickly made the pies for the big toss. Actually, she just threw some chocolate and whipped cream on top of a pastry pan, and called it "pie". Daniel's parents gathered close to the action, but not so close that they would accidentally get hit with any flying objects. Daniel's mom had the camera ready to go.

The nice man stood in his shorts and t-shirt and seemed ready for anything, as Daniel got his pie ready to throw. The whole ninety dollars that he and Noah had accumulated went toward this throw, *so I better make it good*, thought Daniel.

The crowd all counted, "One, Two, Three, Go!"

13

PIE MANIA

Just as Daniel wound up and threw the pie with all his might, the nice old man in his shorts and t-shirt ducked down. SPLAT! The chocolate gooey concoction landed right in the face of the girl who had made the yummy creation.

Daniel heard the click of the camera, and out of the corner of his eye, saw Paige laughing fiercely amongst the crowd. As Daniel realized that Paige was not the only one laughing, he got wailed with a big chocolate and strawberry delight! It was the girl that he had hit accidentally.

Jumping behind the pie-making area, the crowd got involved in the fun. Pies were flying through the air as fast as they could be assembled. The passing cars had to stop since their windshields were covered with sugary, sticky ingredients. The islanders were wildly laughing and ducking, as they proceeded to use up all of the chocolate and whipped cream. Even Daniel's parents were joining in the fun.

When it was all over, Pickle's Deli looked like a baker's kitchen after an explosion. After the crowd finally settled down, someone said, "Hey, where is the guy that was supposed to be hit by the pie?"

Matilda Burns stepped up to the microphone, and said, "You won't believe this, but the gentleman that you all saw duck from the pie just left us a very generous present."

"What is it?" yelled one of the parents in the group.

"Well, let's just say that we will be able to start school sooner than we thought," Matilda happily announced. "The stranger who mysteriously disappeared made sure of that."

Even though the kids were not thrilled to get back to school so soon, they still cheered along with the adults. The energy of the crowd was quite contagious, and the fact that everyone was covered in chocolate and strawberries made it even more so.

"Let's get home and get ourselves cleaned up," Daniel's father said, "we can come back here for the party in a little while."

Daniel's mom put towels on the seats in the car, and they piled in.

"Wait just a second," Daniel told his parents, "I'll be right back." He walked up to Noah, who was getting ready to leave. "Thanks for letting me do the throwing, Noah."

"Sure, no problem," Noah smiled.

"Are you coming back later for the party?" Daniel asked.

"If you are," Noah answered.

"Yeah, I'll see ya later then," Daniel said, and hurried to the car where his parents were waiting for him, with a little bouncier spring in his step.

14

READY FOR THE STORM

The party was a big success, since everyone was still in great spirits from the events of the afternoon. Daniel and Noah spent the whole time together, just relaxing and enjoying all of the delicious food that the people of Coral Bay brought to the party. Daniel realized that day that he already found a great friend on the island, and although no one could ever replace James, Noah sure made it easier to be here.

The two new friends did everything together, and ended up being in the same class. After the first week of school, the people of St. John were well into the beginning of hurricane season.

"Have you ever been in a hurricane?" Daniel asked Noah, as they threw stones into the calm sea.

"Of course. I grew up here. I guess I am used to them, but they can be scary," Noah replied, as he seemed to be remembering something.

"What do you do when the hurricane is here?" Daniel tried not to sound worried as he asked his friend about the unknown.

"Well, you don't leave the house. Just hope that your parents have gotten enough food and supplies to be okay for awhile," Noah explained, "At least your house is strong enough to protect you."

"What do you mean?" Daniel asked, realizing that he had never seen Noah's home.

"Nothing," Noah said, "we better get back inside to class."

That conversation left Daniel wondering about his new friend, as he sat in the classroom daydreaming.

"How about you, Mr. Hawthorne?" Daniel's teacher asked, and then repeated herself. "Daniel? Do you have an answer to my question?"

Daniel shook himself out of his daydream. "Uh, what, Miss Marsh?" He liked his new teacher, and was beginning to understand her better since he was getting used to the West Indian accents.

"Obviously you were not listening, Daniel. Would you like to tell the class what you were thinking about that was so much more important than our lesson?" Miss Marsh asked.

"Hurricanes," Daniel replied without even thinking.

"Interesting. That is actually something you should be thinking about, especially during this time of the year," Miss Marsh said to the class, as well as Daniel. "Are your families all prepared for hurricane season?"

The rest of the day ended up being a little bit more exciting than regular class, since Miss Marsh decided to change the lesson to hurricane preparation. When Daniel got home, that was all that was on his mind.

"Dad, remember when you talked about getting ready for hurricane season?" Daniel asked his father as soon as he saw him.

"Yeah, we're all ready, Daniel. Mom's got all of the food and water packed away, and I stocked up on extra flashlights and candles before the hardware store sold out," Ben Hawthorne explained to his son.

"Well, what about the windows?" Daniel asked, having learned about storm shutters in his class discussion that day.

"All set. A friend of Jonathon's will install hurricane shutters this weekend. He's been busy, since he's the only guy on the island that does it so well. There's nothing to worry about, Daniel, this house is as solid as a rock," his father reassured him.

"How 'bout people who do not have solid homes?" Daniel asked, thinking of what Noah had inferred earlier.

"They usually go somewhere for better protection, or just nail extra wood to the outside of their house," Ben continued. "I wouldn't worry, Daniel. We might not even have any problems this year. Besides, we will always have a warning, since the weather people know far enough in advance."

That night, Daniel thought of James. It seems like it was awhile since he had thought of him, and he felt a little bit guilty about it. He decided to email him a note.

When he got online, he discovered that James had beaten him to it.

Hey D,

You're leaving me hanging. What is going on with the Jumbies there? Did you see one yet? Did you start school yet? I feel like I've already been in school forever. It turns out that Nick is pretty cool after all. I taught him how to play Spy and he's okay at it. Let me know if you'll be coming back to see your grandmother any time soon.

See ya,

J.

He's already replaced me, Daniel thought. Then he realized that he had also made a new friend here on St. John. But Nick was different from Noah. Nick was a jerk. *Well there is nothing that I can do about it,* Daniel decided to himself. *At least James has someone to hang out with.* He wrote back.

Hi J,

Yes, school started, and my teacher's pretty cool. The classes are so much smaller than they were at Salisbury. I haven't seen any Jumbies yet (at least when I'm awake), and hope that I don't ever see one. I'll let you know if I do. We aren't coming back any time soon, so I guess you need to come here. The fishing is great, especially since you can see what you've caught while it's still in the water. I gotta go, but I'll write soon.

Daniel

While shutting down his computer, Daniel thought more about the Jumbies. He wondered why he had not seen one yet. He also remembered that Noah had never finished his story about them, and he had had the opportunity to, many times. He decided to ask him on Monday at school, if he didn't see him over the weekend.

That night Daniel slept soundly, which was good, considering the events that would happen in the days to follow.

15

HERE IT COMES!

Daniel thought it was still dark when he heard his mother call up to him in the loft. "What is it, Mom? I was asleep," he shouted, still feeling slightly groggy.

"The phones are dead, and your father's left for work," his mother's voice sounded shaky. "I think a storm is coming."

"What do you want me to do?" Daniel asked, sitting up in his bed. He saw that the clock said 7:34, so it was already morning. It sure was dark outside.

"I need help getting all of the supplies together, and that guy still hasn't installed the shutters!" his mom was bustling around the kitchen, opening and closing drawers.

When Daniel came downstairs, still in his pajamas, he was able to get a better view of the ominous sky. *It looks strangely quiet out there*, he thought. The clouds appeared to be still, but very dark, and there were no leaves moving on any of the palm trees.

Daniel tried to turn on the television, which barely ever had any reception on a normal day. It did not turn on. "The electricity must be out, Mom," Daniel calmly said, while wondering how that could happen since there was nothing really going on outside.

"Great, now we can't even hear the weather report," Daniel's mom said, with her brow raised up in worry, "I hope your father gets home soon."

It didn't take long before the wind arrived. Daniel and his mother heard some slight blustery sounds outside, then saw that the trees began to move more rapidly.

"We have to get the shutters at least propped up against the windows, Daniel, can you help me?"

Daniel grabbed his sweatshirt and put it on over his pajamas. Apparently, the man that was supposed to install the shutters at least had left them outside the house. Daniel and his mother did the best that they could by lifting them off the ground and leaning them against the windows.

The wind got stronger, and Daniel heard the sliding glass doors actually moving off their tracks. It began to rain.

"That is just not going to do it," Nancy Hawthorne said to her son, just as she heard the car coming quickly down the driveway. "Thank God, your father is home," she said, both relieved and exhausted from trying to get everything ready for the worst.

In walked Daniel's father, who was soaking wet already, with his friend Jonathon behind him. Paige stepped in after her father, looking rather shaken. Daniel wondered what they were doing there, but was grateful for the help. "Just in time, Dad," Daniel said, and then turned to their guests. "How's it going?"

"Terrible," Paige complained, "Since our house is facing the wind, the storm got to it before it even came to this side of the hill. Our whole roof is destroyed."

Paige did not sound like the calm, cool, collected girl that she seemed to be before, Daniel thought, and then asked her, "What happened?"

"Part of our roof is GONE!" Paige started to cry, and Daniel's mother came over to comfort her.

"It's okay, sweetie, your roof can be fixed. The important thing is that you and your father are safe here," Nancy Hawthorne said.

"But the part that blew off is right above my room," Paige could barely speak she was so upset, "all of my stuff will be ruined." Daniel's mother hugged Paige.

"Daniel, come here, quick!" his father yelled from the porch, his voice getting lost in the roar of the wind. "We need help!"

Daniel ran as fast as he could out to the porch, where he found his father and Jonathon trying to nail in the shutters. "Are you strong enough to hold this up, Daniel?" Jonathon asked, handing Daniel the side of the shutter.

"Of course," Daniel said proudly, secretly hoping that Paige would hear him. With all of his might (and the weight of his body), Daniel propped up the shutter so his father could nail it in securely. Jonathon was already working on the next one. *He must be used to this*, thought Daniel.

"BEN, HELP!" Jonathon's shouts could barely be heard, since the wind had picked up tremendously.

All that they could hear was the loud banging of wood hitting wood.

16

QUITE A HEADACHE

At that point, Daniel, Ben, and Jonathon could hardly see each other since the rain whipped into their eyes.

"What happened, Jonathon?" Ben shouted.

"Look!" Jonathon replied, pointing down the hill.

Finally, they saw what he was trying to tell them all along. One of the main shutters had blown off the deck and slammed into a large tree, shattering it into pieces.

Daniel began to shake, but tried to remain brave. "Dad, what are we gonna do?"

"Just get inside now, we'll handle it." Ben's voice quivered slightly.

"I'm not leaving you out here," Daniel said stubbornly.

"NOW!" Ben screamed, as he pointed toward the house.

Daniel didn't have to be told again. He ran inside, anxious to tell his mother and Paige what was going on outside.

Meanwhile, the two men fought to stay on the deck, since the wind was so strong it felt as if it would pick them up and toss them away.

"Ben, just help me get this last one on, then we have to go inside. We'll deal with the missing shutter later," Jonathon said as loudly as he could, while he struggled to hold up the last remaining shutter.

They managed to secure the window, leaving a patch where the last shutter should have been. As they were heading back inside through the rear door, a large branch fell hard from a tree and knocked Ben Hawthorne down on the ground before he knew what hit him.

Inside the house, the other three were anxiously waiting for the men to return. "I feel so helpless since there is nothing left to do in here," Nancy said nervously, "I hope everything is okay, they seem to be taking–"

She got cut off. Jonathon stormed in, shouting for the others to help him quickly. It all happened so fast; Daniel could hardly conceive of what was going on. The wind was whipping furiously around them, as they gathered their strength to lift Ben off the ground. He seemed to be out cold.

When they brought him in the house and placed him on the couch, he still did not move.

Daniel spoke first. "Is he going to be all right?" he asked no one in particular.

Jonathon took over. "Yes, Daniel, he just got the wind knocked out of him—literally. Let's get him some blankets."

The four of them bustled about the villa, finding blankets and trying to remain calm. Nancy Hawthorne kept looking over at the couch, hoping to see movement.

"What's all of this noise? I have an aching headache." It was Ben, waking up in the midst of the confusion.

"Thank God!" Nancy shouted, running over to her husband. "Are you okay? How do you feel? Do you need an ambulance?"

Ben interrupted, "Please calm down, honey, I'm fine. It's the house I am worried about. The storm seems to be getting worse."

"It's more than a storm at this point," Jonathon chimed in. "The hurricane has arrived."

17

THE WAIT

Daniel went up to his room to gather himself together. *Dad could have been really hurt*, he thought, *and I didn't even know what to do to help him.* It also didn't seem as if there were any ambulances on the island either, which was a little scary for Daniel to think about. As he plopped down on his bed, he realized that he was still wearing his pajamas. He hoped that Paige hadn't noticed.

After hearing more loud bangs from outside the house, Daniel decided he'd rather be with the rest of his family. He thought of Noah and once again wondered what kind of house he lived in.

Downstairs was even louder. Every few seconds, the wind could be heard whistling, as though it was making a trip right through the center of the house. The skies had darkened more, so the candles were burning, as the others sat around the kitchen table. Daniel's Dad was holding an ice pack on his head.

They were talking about the space where the destroyed shutter should have been. "It looks like you might be all right, Ben," Jonathon stated, "the wind does not seem to be blowing in that direction at all."

"What do we do, now?" Ben asked his friend, as everyone listened.

"At this point, we just wait. I know it sounds crazy, but that's all we can do."

"We can also hope that everyone else on the island is okay," Nancy added.

So, as the day turned into night, the violent winds continued, and the pounding torrent could still be heard upon the aluminum roof. When it was time for bed, Daniel just wanted to crawl up to his bedroom haven and go to sleep. His mother had a different plan.

"Daniel, honey, why don't you help me get your room ready for Jonathon and Paige?" she asked gently.

Trying not to look too surprised, Daniel nodded.

"The couch isn't so bad," his Mom whispered to him as they climbed up to the loft with clean sheets.

"Easy for you to say, Mom," Daniel grumbled to himself, but also aloud.

10

DA BIG BLOW

It turned out that the couch wasn't what was "so bad" that night. It was the howling winds, the crashing noises, the loud pelting rain, and the complete lack of sleep.

Daniel tried every position possible in an attempt to get comfortable, to no avail. As he lay there wishing he could at least watch TV, he thought about how much his life had changed in the last few weeks. He had gone from living in a comfy house in Connecticut to fearing for his life and the life of his family.

Just then, Daniel's Dad shuffled into the living room, holding his head.

"Are you okay, Dad?"

"Yeah, it's just the pounding headache and the dreadful noise that's bugging me." He headed into the kitchen to grab some aspirin and a bottle of water, and continued to speak to Daniel. "How 'bout you? Is the couch working for you?"

"If you mean am I sleeping, then NO," Daniel replied. He paused for a moment, and then said, "Dad?"

"Yes, son?"

"I'm sort of scared."

Ben sat down next to Daniel on the couch, scooting Daniel's legs over so he could fit. "You mean of the storm?"

"It's a little more than a storm, Dad, it's a HURRICANE. I've never been in one before, and it makes a lot of scary noises."

"Well, Daniel, I've never been in one either, and I'll have to agree with you, it is a little unsettling." His father continued, "I am just glad that we are all together, and that our friends have a place to stay that is safe."

"Is it?" Daniel peered at his father from under a sheet, that was beginning to get damp from the humidity in the house.

"Is it what, Dan?"

"Safe?" Daniel asked.

"As safe as it can be right now. Let's hope that it stays that way." As he ran his hand through his salt-and-pepper colored hair, Ben Hawthorne silently hoped that everything would be all right for his family. He was a little more concerned about it than he had let on to his son.

"Why don't you try to get some sleep, Daniel? It's going to be a long day tomorrow." And, patting his son's leg before he got up off the couch, Ben Hawthorne shuffled back to his bed, ice pack in tow.

Daniel stayed on the couch, looking up at the ceiling. Just as his eyes began to blink slowly, a crashing sound came from outside, and jolted him awake. *Thunder*, he thought. *Just what I need.* As he glanced outside through the space that the missing shutter had created, he saw flashes of lightning.

He quickly looked back outside again. He thought he spotted something other than what was familiar to him. As another bolt of lightning flashed, Daniel saw an outline of what looked like a large person. He couldn't believe his eyes. *It must be because I am so tired*, Daniel thought to himself. *There is no way that a person can be that big!*

But, as he dared to look again, Daniel could definitely make out the shape of something enormous, that was moving toward him. The room became very warm, and he could not take his eyes off of this strange being that seemed to be gliding right through the glass door.

Daniel held his hand in front of his eyes to keep the blinding light from shining into them. He was shaking so much, he could not move. Nothing came out of his mouth when he tried to speak.

Between the noisy hammering rain and the sound of crackling thunder, Daniel could not think clearly. The flash of light became so bright that the last thing that Daniel remembered feeling was a cold wind whipping through him, then darkness.

19

ALL OVER

Daniel awoke abruptly to the sound of whispering voices.
"What time is it?" he asked, as his eyes adjusted to the
light coming from the kitchen.

"Sorry, honey, it's early. We didn't want to wake you, but
we had to check everything out." It was his mother, who stood
next to Paige and Jonathon.

As Daniel thought about how awkward it was to be lying
there in his PJ's while a girl from his school sat in his kitchen,
he suddenly had a memory that made him shiver. *Was that
another nightmare or did it really happen? It seemed so real.*

"Daniel, are you OKAY?" his mother had come to sit on
the couch with him.

"Oh, uh, yeah. Just tired. I don't hear anything outside
any more. Is it over?" he asked his Mom.

"I hope so. It looks that way," his mother answered, with her face scrunched up the way it did when she was worried about something.

"How's Dad?"

"Not so good. He is still in bed with a headache. He should be fine after a little more rest. Don't worry."

Daniel knew better. It took a lot for his father to stay in bed. *If only we were back in Connecticut, there would be a decent doctor to look after my Dad. Then again, none of this would have happened if we had been back where we belong*, Daniel thought, as he wrapped the sheet around himself hoping to take the chill out of the air.

He needed some time to take in everything that had happened to him. He secretly wished that they did not have company. Paige seemed to read his mind.

"Sorry we are in your way, Daniel," she said. "We'll be leaving as soon as my Dad can clear out the driveway."

"No big deal." Then, almost as an afterthought, Daniel said, "I hope your room is okay when you get back to your house."

"Thanks, I do too."

A couple of hours later, Paige and her father were able to get out of the driveway, thanks to their four-wheel drive vehicle and a little determination.

By that time, Ben Hawthorne was up and about and seemed to be feeling a little better. The entire area around the outside of the house was a complete mess, and would take a very long time to clean up.

"It looks like we might have to wait on that pool," Ben said to his wife.

Daniel didn't care. All he could think about was what had happened the night before, when he was all alone. *No one would ever believe me,* he thought. *Except for maybe Noah.* He couldn't help but think that his new friend might be in some sort of trouble. Every time Daniel had asked him about where he lived, Noah had seemed to change the subject.

With the phone lines down and the roads torn up from the storm, it would be quite awhile before Daniel would find out about his friend.

20

CLEAN UP TIME

School would not be opened again for weeks. There simply were not enough people on the island to get things together fast enough. Miss Marsh's home was not far from Noah's, and before long, word got around the small community that some houses in that area were completely destroyed by the hurricane.

Daniel was crushed. It seemed that ever since they had arrived in St. John, nothing had gone right. He had to find Noah and see if he and his mother were okay. He was quick to volunteer to go with Ben on errands that day. It would be the first time they could venture out after the storm had washed away a lot of the streets. It took longer than usual to get to Pickle's Deli.

"Dad, have you heard anything else about the people who lost their homes?" he asked as they got out of their car.

"We'll soon find out," Ben said, as he slammed the door shut. "If anyone knows, it's Matilda."

Ben was right. Matilda had all of the answers. Daniel couldn't help but wonder how news travelled so fast without working telephones. He caught the middle of the conversation as he heard Matilda's voice.

"...they both have to be completely rebuilt. The families don't have the money to do it themselves, so some of us from Coral Bay decided to give them a hand," Matilda continued, as she leaned over the counter to hand Ben an iced tea and Daniel a cold root beer. The weather was back to normal again; as hot as ever.

"Count us in. We'll head over there right now and see what they need." They were back in the car as Ben waved to Matilda and drove off.

It was difficult to get up the hill, but Ben Hawthorne was determined and recognized a couple of Jeeps when he got to a very steep driveway.

"I guess we walk from here, Daniel. Are you up for it?"

Looking up at his father and rolling his eyes, Daniel asked, "Dad, it's more like are YOU up for it. Don't you remember what happened to your head?"

"I'm okay, son. Just a little headache. These people need our help, so I'll manage just fine."

Daniel was scared of what they might see when they turned the corner. Not only was he still shaken up about his possible encounter with a Jumbie, but he was concerned that Noah and his family might be hurt.

The answer to his question came sooner than he thought. In the midst of the teacher's destroyed house, was Noah, carrying a large armful of wood across a muddy front yard.

"Noah!" Daniel shouted to his friend and darted toward him. "Are you all right?"

"Sure, why wouldn't I be?" Noah smiled, handing half of the wood to Daniel. "Can you help me take these over to the guys? They are trying to fix one of the rooms that was ruined in the storm."

"Why does everyone keep calling it a 'storm'? It seems to me like we had the first hurricane of the season, and hopefully the last," Daniel said.

"You're right. It was pretty bad. I mean, look at this place." Noah continued, "Luckily, Miss Marsh's neighbor didn't get hit as hard, and they have plenty of help over there anyway."

Daniel glanced around. He had never thought he would see such destruction from a force of nature. Miss Marsh's entire house needed to be repaired, and it seemed as if the whole town of Coral Bay was there to help her.

As Daniel and Noah pitched in to help the men repair the house, they swapped stories of what it had been like to be in the hurricane less than two weeks before. It turned out that Noah had not had as rough of a time as Daniel, and as they talked about their homes, Daniel became even more curious about what might have happened to Noah's house.

"Do you wanna go see it? I'm getting hungry anyway. And it looks like I'm not the only one." Noah said, as he looked up at the other helpers munching on some sandwiches that Matilda had packed for them at Pickle's.

"Yeah, just let me tell my dad," Daniel said, not wanting him to worry. Since Ben could not be found, Daniel decided that they wouldn't be gone for too long, so he followed Noah down the driveway and into the washed out muddy road.

21

TELLING NOAH

It took the boys about twenty minutes to get to Noah's driveway, especially since they had to dodge the fallen rocks and navigate the muddy pathways. While they hiked up the hill, Daniel tried to figure out a way to not seem surprised by Noah's run down house. With the way Noah had been avoiding questions about it, Daniel had a feeling that Noah must be embarrassed.

This thought was quickly out of Daniel's mind when he finally caught a glimpse of Noah's home. As they reached the top of the driveway, Daniel first noticed the view of the harbor below, as well as many more islands than he could see from his own house. It was then that he spotted the huge oval-shaped swimming pool, and the endless vines of bright pink bougainvillea, which enveloped the biggest house that Daniel had ever seen.

"This is all yours?" Daniel asked, holding back no surprise whatsoever.

"Well, mine and my mom's," Noah said, in the same embarrassed tone that he had used before.

"Wow. It's so...so...nice." Daniel could not believe his eyes, as Noah led him in through the immense carved wooden front door. The first greeting they had as they entered the house was from a limping brown dog, who seemed quite happy to see Noah.

"Hey, Scamp!" Noah said excitedly, as he grabbed his dog around the neck and pet the top of his head. "This is Daniel, he's okay," Noah told his pup.

Daniel carefully put out his hand, with his palm facing upward, as he learned to do when meeting an unfamiliar pet. "What happened to his leg?" he asked, noticing that Scamp was balancing on three legs.

"He got hit by a car. He was a stray, and I found him in the road and took care of him until he healed," Noah explained, "and we've kept him ever since."

"Is that you, Noah?" his mom was heard asking from the kitchen area.

"Yeah, Mom, and Daniel too. We're here for lunch."

"Yes, sir," Noah's mom smiled as she appeared in the doorway. "Hi, Daniel, how'd you fare in the storm?"

"Hurricane, Mom. Daniel doesn't like it when you call it a 'storm'."

"I don't care, Noah," Daniel quickly said, then turned to address Noah's mother. "We did okay, except my dad got hit by a branch and got knocked out. He's alright now."

"Well I'm glad he's okay! Tell him to take it easy. Those hurricanes can be very dangerous. How's it going over at Miss Marsh's?"

"Pretty good, there are a lot of people there to help. We are hungry, though," Noah hinted once again.

"I can take a hint, come into the kitchen and I'll feed you two hard workers," Noah's mom said as she turned and headed for the fridge.

Daniel borrowed Miss Walter's cell phone to let his mom know where he was in case his parents were worried. He left her a message and quickly went outside to find Noah.

As the two friends sat alone on the large patio overlooking the Caribbean Sea, Daniel bit into a delicious ham sandwich and took a sip of lemonade as he decided to tell Noah about his latest Jumbie experience.

"I think I might have met a Jumbie," was all that came out of his mouth.

"What?"

"You heard me, I saw a Jumbie! It was the night of the hurricane, and I was sleeping on the couch." Daniel stopped to take another bite.

"Well, what did it look like?" Noah asked, even though he knew all about Jumbies. It was never too much to hear more.

"It was much bigger than a person, but it didn't look like a person. It was like a shape of light, and it could move through walls and stuff." Daniel shuddered as he tried to remember more about the night he had been trying to forget.

"Yep, that sounds like a Jumbie. I can't believe you just moved here and were already visited." Noah began to lower his voice, not wanting his mother to hear their conversation. "Were you scared?"

Daniel began to say, "No," but realized that it wouldn't do any good to fib to Noah. "I was pretty scared," he said instead. "And before the Jumbie left the room, or wherever it went, it got so cold that I was shaking."

"This was in your living room?" Noah asked, apparently thinking about something.

"Yeah."

"We'll just have to keep the Jumbie from returning to your house," Noah declared, as if it was as easy as wishing it wouldn't happen again.

"We can do that?" Daniel asked. "How?"

"I'll show you," Noah told his friend, "just as soon as we can be there without any adults."

22

A FAMILIAR FACE

Daniel and Noah ended up going back to school soon after their talk on Noah's patio. There had not been any chance for them to be alone to plan their attack on the Jumbies, and luckily neither one of them had any "visits" since the hurricane.

Daniel sat in class, staring out of the window as he vaguely heard his teacher, Miss Marsh, thanking them all for their help.

"...and if it hadn't been for you great kids and your families, I would not be here to teach you today. I have been trying to think of a way to thank you, and I know there is nothing I can do to make up for all of your kindness. However, I made you each something as a token of my appreciation..."

Just then, Miss Marsh passed by Daniel and placed a handmade bracelet on his desk. It was made of a thin beige rope and had three different colored beads woven into it.

Daniel thought it was pretty cool for a bracelet, and wrapped it around his wrist.

As he looked over at Noah who sat two rows away from him, he noticed that Noah was glancing out of the classroom door. Daniel mouthed to him, "Who's out there?"

"What?" Noah mouthed back.

"Is it a Jumbie?" Daniel asked quietly, knowing that Noah would definitely be able to read his lips for that word.

As Noah was trying to explain who he saw without getting in trouble, Miss Marsh stood up and asked the class for their attention. "I would like to introduce you to a very special gentleman. You all know how we have gone for so long without a principal. We also talked about how very important it is for every school to have a principal. Well, our school finally does!"

She stopped and smoothed her Caribbean colored skirt, then motioned for the mystery man to come into the classroom. "Boys and Girls, I'd like you to meet your new principal, Mr. Denby."

Daniel's jaw dropped. Mr. Denby was the nice old man from the pie-throwing contest who had mysteriously disappeared! He was the same man who had caused the whole town of Coral Bay to cover Pickle's Deli in chocolate and strawberry goodness. Not only that, but he was also the man who had secretly left money for the school to open. Mr. Denby seemed to recognize Daniel as the one who was supposed to smash a pie in his face.

"Hello, class, I see that some of you already know who I am," Mr. Denby said while smiling. "I am honored to be a part of this great school, and I look forward to getting to know each and every one of you." Then, looking at his watch, Mr. Denby waved to the class and left the room.

Is anything normal around here? Would James ever believe any of this? Daniel continued to daydream until the end of the day, wondering if he would ever get used to all of the crazy things that go on in St. John. And while looking out the window at the lemon trees, Daniel bravely allowed his mind to remember the visit that he had had from the Jumbie on that frightful night.

23

THE PLAN

Autumn came and went and no one in Daniel's family really acknowledged its passing except for knowing they were safely out of hurricane season. As Noah told Daniel while they sat in their secret fort, "You know what they say about the hurricane season in the Caribbean: 'June, too soon; July, stand by; August, come they must; September, remember; October, all over'."

Daniel laughed. "That's good, 'cause I'm kind of sick of worrying about when the next hurricane is coming."

"I know what you mean. Now we don't have to think about it until next year," Noah said, sounding relieved. "I can't believe we got through the season with only one big one and a couple of little storms."

"Well right now I would be freezing cold if we still lived in Connecticut," Daniel told his friend. "I can't believe it's November already. My grandmother is coming for Thanksgiving and she will probably love this place."

"It sounds like you might like it a little bit more than when you got here," Noah observed aloud.

Although Daniel did not want to admit it, Noah was right. He was beginning to like his new home and was even feeling more comfortable in his surroundings. He just wished that he didn't have to feel so guilty about it. James used to be his best friend and now it had been weeks since they'd even emailed each other.

Noah snapped Daniel back into reality. "Are we still on for this Saturday?"

Daniel had been afraid of this for months now. They were finally going to make sure there would be no more Jumbie visits at Daniel's house again. While nothing had happened since the hurricane, Daniel was hoping they could just forget about it, but Noah insisted. Daniel just didn't want to remind the Jumbies where he lived.

"We're going to need Paige's help," Noah told Daniel. "I hope that's not going to be a problem with you liking her and all."

"Me…what?" Daniel didn't know what to say, as his face turned a deep shade of pink. "I don't like her; she's a girl. Besides, the only reason I hang out with her at all is because our fathers work together."

"Whatever you say, but we still need her help." Noah turned away to smile to himself.

"That's fine. As long as she doesn't tell anyone about our plan."

24

DA JUMBIE SOON COME

The sun had just finished setting when Daniel heard a tap on the kitchen window. It was Saturday night, and Daniel's parents had finally gone out to dinner without dragging him along. The only way for the plan to work was if it happened after dark, so Daniel and Noah had been waiting for the perfect opportunity.

"Is that you, Noah?" Daniel whispered through the screen, since he could not see anyone.

Up popped two heads, with Noah's nose pressing against the screen. "Who else do you think it would be? A Jumbie?"

Seeing Paige, Daniel opted to be brave. "Of course not, I was just making sure that my parents hadn't come back. Come on in."

When Daniel's two friends walked in to the kitchen, Noah unloaded a grocery bag onto the table, and Paige looked around, as if she expected to see someone else.

"Are you sure we won't get in trouble for doing this?" she asked the other two.

"Don't worry about it, Paige," Noah calmed her down. "We have no choice anyway. If we get caught, we'll just say we're playing some sort of game."

"Yeah, fun game, making me do this with you two. I don't have much time before I have to sneak back into the house, so make it quick."

"Yes, ma'am!" Noah snapped, as he prepared the contents for ridding the house of Jumbies.

Daniel quietly took it all in as he watched Noah fish through the ingredients for Jumbie removal. A container of salt, a box of rice, a bottle of dishwashing detergent, matchbooks, candles, and a jar of honey. Noah was reading off a crumpled up note to himself, as if there was no one else in the room. *This is serious stuff*, Daniel thought. *It sure takes a lot of concentration.*

"Ready!" Noah shouted, taking the role of this particular project seriously.

"What are we supposed to do?" Paige asked, slightly quivering.

"First make sure there is not one light on in the house," Noah said, and Paige and Daniel went around each room, turning off the lights. Noah stayed back to light the candles so they would be able to see well.

They returned to the living room, to find Noah crouching down in the corner, placing a candle on the floor and pouring a tablespoon of honey right next to it.

"Great, my mom will love this," Daniel said sarcastically, thinking that maybe this wasn't such a good idea after all. "What is the honey for?"

"It should help attract the Jumbies to the corners of the room, after we sprinkle salt on top of the honey. It's important to use the same amount of salt and honey in each corner, and to leave a candle burning in all of the corners as well."

"How do you know all of this stuff?" Paige asked, while glancing at the door that would take her out of this suddenly ominous room.

"Plenty of practice. After I did this at my house, there hasn't been a Jumbie since. The only thing is, I didn't want to do it alone again, since there is no way to guarantee what will happen."

"I...I don't know about this, Noah. If my parents come home and see this, I will definitely be in trouble. Maybe we should–"

Noah cut Daniel off. "Too late now, Daniel. We're almost ready to start. You will be glad when this is over. Now both of you grab a candle and do the same thing I just did, in each corner." He then proceeded to take the dishwashing soap and make large "S" shapes all over the living room floor.

"Now what are you doing?" Daniel was horrified; picturing what would happen if his parents walked in the door right now.

"People believe that the soap will cleanse the house of Jumbies, and the 'S' shape is for 'spirits', which is what the Jumbies like to be called." After Noah seemed satisfied with the amount of S's in the room, he stopped and said, "Now we sit on the couch and wait."

Paige grabbed one of her braids, and tugged. "I almost hate to ask this, but what are we waiting for?"

"The Jumbies, of course, silly...geez, don't you listen?" Noah seemed to be getting irritated, and slightly nervous about what might happen, especially since he was supposed to be the expert. "Oh, I almost forgot," Noah quickly said, and grabbed the box of rice.

"What is that for? How much stuff do you need for this?" asked Daniel.

Noah took a deep breath, then exhaled impatiently. "Some people believe that if you throw rice on the ground, the Jumbies have to stop and count it before they attack."

"ATTACK?" yelled both Daniel and Paige at the same time.

"Don't worry, trust me. This is just to cover all the bases. Now will you please sit down," said Noah, sounding more frustrated than before.

The three terrified friends sat on the couch, watching the four candles in the corners of the room. Daniel didn't feel like talking, but the silence was just too much to bear. "What's next?"

"We wait," Noah whispered. "It's probably best if we don't talk, since we don't want to scare the Jumbies when they come."

Just then, a large shadow went shooting across the floor, and Paige shrieked. "I can't take this, I'm leaving. Good luck," and she was out the door before they could tell her that what had made her scream was a very large and quite harmless gecko.

25

DE-JUMBIE RECIPE

Noah shrugged his shoulders, and said, "That's what I get for asking your girlfriend to help."

"She's not my–" but Daniel was interrupted.

Suddenly, a cold wind came through the living room and whipped away Daniel's words. He wrapped his arms around himself to keep the chill away, but nothing could stop him from shaking.

"Don't move!" was all Daniel could hear Noah say, and then, following the source of the wind, Daniel looked up. He had to hold his hand in front of his eyes to block out the intense bright light that was streaming down upon him.

"NOAH! What is…?"

"SHHHHH!" Noah snapped back. "Just wait!"

Wait? Was his friend crazy? Even so, Daniel was so afraid he could not move anyway, so he stayed put.

The light seemed to become stronger and brighter as all four candles blew out at once. Daniel felt something that might have been hands around his neck. He suddenly could not catch his breath, and then the "hands" released their pressure. In what seemed like a split second, the room came back to normal. Except it was dark.

Noah was the only one who seemed able to move, so he went about the room turning on as many lights as he could find.

"They're gone, Daniel, you can breathe now."

"Wh—What just happened?" Daniel still felt a chill.

"We did it! Look, the stuff is all gone, and…wait," Noah pointed to the floor, "look at what they left for us."

Daniel looked down, and on the floor, where there used to be S's, was a message written in dishwashing soap. It said, simply, "NOT BAD".

"Not bad? What is that supposed to mean?" Daniel rubbed his eyes to make sure he was seeing clearly.

"I guess they thought we did a good job of scaring them away," Noah said proudly.

"Scaring who away?" Daniel's mom asked, already standing in the kitchen with Ben.

Daniel looked down to the floor. *Great*, he thought, *now how am I going to explain the soap all over the place?* "We're just playing a game with soap, no big deal, I'll clean it up."

"Clean what up, honey?" she asked, her eyes widening.

Daniel and Noah looked at each other. It seemed that they both realized something at the same time; Daniel's parents were not able to see any of this.

"I better get going," Noah said with a smile, "it must be late. See ya." And on his way out the door, he said good night to Daniel's parents.

"Good night, Noah," Nancy and Ben both said, then Ben's nose made a sniffling sound. He turned to Daniel and asked sternly, "Daniel, what were you and Noah really up to? I think I smell smoke."

Daniel hung his head low. "It's a long story, Dad, but remember how we talked about Jumbies? Well, we were trying to get rid of them so they don't come back." *I knew that I shouldn't have listened to Noah*, he thought. *Now I am in trouble.*

"Come back? What is that supposed to mean? Listen, young man, you have no reason to ever play with matches, do you understand me?" Ben was furious.

"I know, Dad, you are right. I promise not to light anything again."

Ben and Nancy glanced at each other, and Nancy looked worried. Ben continued, "I know you won't, Daniel, but just to make sure, you are grounded for a week. You are old enough to know that you should never touch matches. You apparently have no idea how dangerous they are."

"But Dad–" Daniel started, but the look on his parents' faces said it all. Daniel turned around and yelled out, "You don't understand!" He then climbed up his ladder as fast as he could. "I'm going to sleep", he shouted downstairs, and flopped onto his comfy bed, completely exhausted.

26

GRANDMA'S ON ISLAND

Thanksgiving came around soon after Daniel had spent a week grounded in his room, and it was time for Grandma to come to the island for a visit. Daniel was so excited to show his grandmother around the island, he volunteered to go with his parents to meet her at the ferry.

As the Hawthorne family stood on the platform, Daniel could already see some people waving from the distance. As the ferry got closer, he recognized the blue and white floral pattern of a very familiar dress; it was Grandma! Her bright smile could be seen for miles, and as she waved to the family, Daniel realized how happy he was that she was here. *The only one missing now is James*, he thought.

"Hi sweetie!" she shouted, as she put her bags down and ran to give her grandson the first hug. "I've missed you all so," she said, and continued to dole out hugs.

"We've missed you too, Grandma. Wait until you see this place. You'll love it." Daniel didn't notice the looks and smiles between the adults as he grabbed his grandmother's hand and walked her to the Jeep, talking the entire way.

After the short version of the St. John tour, they all went back to the house. It was already getting late, and Daniel had so much more to tell his grandmother.

"It can wait, Daniel. Grandma had a long trip," Ben told his son. "Why don't you go up and get your room ready so we can all get some sleep? Mom and I will take your room so Grandma will be comfortable in ours."

Great, Daniel thought, *that means I get the couch again.* He hadn't slept on the couch since the hurricane, and he remembered quite well what had happened that time. Since no one would understand, he told his father, "I just need a minute, then my room is all yours," and quickly climbed up his ladder.

When he reached his room, he went right for the computer. It had been awhile since he had heard from James, and he thought it would be good to email him.

James,

What's up with you? I haven't seen any emails from you lately. My grandmother just got here, and we are having a big Thanksgiving meal on Thursday. I didn't get to tell you that we chased the Jumbies away. It's a long story, but my friend Noah knows a lot about them and he helped me get rid of them, even though he got me in trouble... The Jumbies even left us a message that we did a good job! I gotta run since my parents are sleeping in my room, but write soon and let me know what is going on there.

Daniel

That night on the couch, Daniel tossed and turned and could not stop thinking about the last time he had tried to sleep in the living room. But it seemed like only a few minutes passed before the kitchen was filled with the scent of bacon and coffee, and the sound of comforting voices. He decided he might as well get up, so he ran upstairs to get dressed and checked his computer while he was there. It turns out that Daniel was not the only one who tossed and turned the night before.

Hey Dan,

I got up in the middle of the night since I couldn't sleep and there was your email! It's good to hear that you got rid of the Jumbies, although I'd like to see one if I can ever get there to visit (I would not mind getting a look at a sea turtle too, how cool). School is the same, except I joined the soccer team with Nick and we will have a lot of practices that start in the spring. We have a long winter break this year, and I'm just going to be at home. I wish you could be here since there has been a lot of snow—we could be sledding on Cemetery Hill. I have to go, but write soon if you can.

–James

Daniel sat back on his chair. *Sledding.* He had forgotten all about that. It was so warm and sunny outside, that the cold had completely slipped his mind. He and James used to go sledding almost every weekend in the winter, and as much as they could after school. Daniel had not allowed himself to think about all of the things that he missed about his old home. *Then again*, he thought, *I'm not having such a bad time here, either.*

After getting dressed, Daniel shinnied down his ladder and joined his family for his grandmother's visit, which would only last a short week.

27

CARNIVAL SOON COME

The rest of the school year passed slowly, just as it did in Connecticut. Daniel's days were filled with homework, bike riding, swimming, and secret meetings in the fort at Jumbie Beach. A lot of what was happening in the fort had to do with the upcoming event of the summer, maybe even the year. It was called Carnival, and everyone was talking about it.

"Tell me again about why you have this Carnival," Daniel asked Noah, as he sat petting Scamp in their secret hiding place.

"Geez, do you ever listen? It has been a West Indian tradition for many years, and now all of the people of the island are included," Noah continued. "It's just like a parade, except there is also a big party which lasts for at least three days. We have it to celebrate life and our culture. We also do it to show the Jumbies that we can be friends."

"How do you do that?" Daniel was glued to his friend's every word.

"Well, mostly us kids dress up like Jumbies."

"You dress like a big figure of light?"

"No, silly, we dress like spirits. With bright costumes and makeup. And we walk on stilts."

"Wow, that must be hard."

"Yeah, that's why we start practicing a couple of months before Carnival."

"Can I be in it too?" Daniel asked.

"Of course. You're a 'local' now. I'll show you how it's done."

When Daniel went home that day, he was so excited about learning how to walk on stilts; he barely noticed the activity happening in his back yard. When he heard the machinery, he walked out onto the deck to see what was going on. All he saw was a man on a bulldozer (must be Dozer Tom), his father, and Jonathon. *The pool! They must be putting in the pool for the summer!* Daniel couldn't believe they hadn't told him.

His mom came out to join him on the deck. "We were hoping to surprise you, Daniel, but now that they've started the building process, it's kind of hard to keep it from you."

"I know! I can't wait, thanks, Mom," Daniel said, while hugging his mother.

"I'm glad you are happy about it, Daniel, I know how much you've been missing your grandmother."

"What?" Daniel couldn't figure out what Grandma had to do with a pool.

"Well, the cottage should only take about a month to build since it is small, but it will be a perfect size for your grandmother to have some privacy."

"You mean when she comes to visit? So I won't have to give up my room?"

"No…oh, Daniel, you really don't know. Grandma has decided to join us here. To live."

Daniel couldn't tell how he was feeling. He had been so excited about the pool, but this was good news too. *Great news, actually.*

"For good?"

"Yes, Daniel, she loved it here when she visited over Thanksgiving. We finally talked her into it. Isn't it great?"

"Yeah, it is," Daniel said, and realized that he was truly happy about the news. *A pool is no big deal, anyway.*

20

GIRLS ALLOWED?

While the cottage for Grandma was being built, Daniel and Noah continued to plan for the summer. Daniel was especially looking forward to sailing lessons, and was very curious about the events of Carnival. One day the two friends were discussing their ideas in the fort, when they heard a strange sound coming from the bushes.

"What was that?" Daniel asked.

"Probably the usual animal that lives around here, maybe a lizard, or a snake," Noah replied, while keeping busy carving a long piece of wood.

"A snake?" Paige replied from the bush, showing her face. "Where?"

Noah rolled his eyes, as Daniel asked her, "How did you find this place?"

"I've always known it was here. I just figured it was a boys' thing, so I left you alone," Paige said, as she continued to approach the fort.

"Good idea," Noah said. "What made you change your mind?"

"Thanks a lot, I just wanted to see what you were up to. It's not like this island is filled with girls my age to hang out with."

Daniel felt bad for Paige, and told her, "It's okay, you can come on in."

Noah shot him a look, and turned to Paige and said, "On one condition. Can you sew?"

"Kind of. Why?"

"Daniel needs a costume for Carnival. We are working on the stilts, and I need someone to sew the material together for the top of the Jumbie."

"You're still going to be a Jumbie, after what happened?" Paige asked, as Daniel thought, *you don't know the half of it.* He still thought that they should have told Paige the whole story, but Noah did not think it was a good idea to tell anyone.

"Of course we are. You weren't even there to see what happened. They actually complimented us on doing a good job of getting rid of them," Noah told Paige.

"What are you talking about?" she asked, looking at Daniel.

"Never mind," Noah said without looking up. "Do you want to help or not?"

Embarrassed that his friend was treating Paige so badly, Daniel chimed in. "We can tell her, Noah. It's no big deal." Then, turning to Paige, he could not help but notice her honey blonde hair, and the way that her pretty face seems to light up when she talks. "The Jumbies left us a message after you left. It said, 'Not Bad'."

Paige did not miss Daniel's glances, and smiled as his cheeks turned the familiar shade of pink. "What does that mean, anyway?" she asked.

"We think it means that the Jumbies believe we did a good job of trying to scare them. Unless they're just messing with us," Daniel told Paige, wanting her to be included, but trying not to make Noah mad at the same time.

"Well I don't mind sewing you an outfit, Daniel. I think it's a great idea to show the Jumbies that you think they are good. At least it can't hurt."

"Thanks, Paige," Daniel said, "I better get going. My mom will be here to pick me up any minute." Then, grabbing a sea grape off of the bush, he popped it in his mouth and waved to his island friends as he headed toward the white sandy beach.

29

GOOD JUMBIES?

Carnival was going to happen in two weeks, and Daniel had not gotten to practice walking on stilts yet. It turned out that his father and Jonathon needed help with the cottage, because Grandma was coming in time for the anticipated celebration, and they were running behind.

Since school was over for the year, Daniel could not exactly avoid being recruited to help, so he did, with Jumbies on his mind.

As he handed his father a hammer, Daniel drifted into a daydream. *This is my chance to show the Jumbies that I want to be their friend,* he thought. *They are not going to scare me anymore, especially after I let them know that I think they aren't so bad.*

"That's IT!" Daniel shouted to no one in particular.

Jonathon and Ben looked at each other, raising their eyebrows. "What's it, son?" Ben asked, while still concentrating on his task at hand.

"I...I have to go. I'll be back later," and leaving no time for any response, Daniel turned on his heels and dashed out of the cottage.

He got right on his bike and coasted all the way down to Jumbie Beach, where he knew he would find Noah. It seemed that it took forever to get there, especially since he had to be careful of the cars, which drove pretty fast on the island's winding roads.

When he finally got to the hiding place, he could not contain his disappointment when the only person he saw was Paige, carefully sewing his costume.

"Oh, hi. That looks good. Have you seen Noah?" Daniel was still catching his breath.

"Yeah, he was here awhile ago but he got called away. I think he went down town to talk to the parade coordinators," Paige said, while looking up from her work. She could see that Daniel was in a hurry. "Is something wrong?" she asked.

"Well, actually..."

"Hey, Daniel, what's up?" Noah entered the fort just in time.

Daniel paused for a moment, not sure if he could share this revelation with Paige present, then realized it was okay. "I was helping out with the cottage, it's almost finished, and I think I figured something out."

"Don't keep us hanging," Noah said, sounding curious.

"Remember when we got the message from the Jumbies that said, 'Not Bad'?"

"Of course I remember. How could I forget that day?" Noah chuckled.

"I can't believe we didn't think of this sooner, but I'm pretty sure they were talking about themselves." Then, seeing the perplexed looks on his friends' faces, Daniel said, "The

Jumbies *aren't* bad, don't you see? They wanted us to know that they are *good*, not *bad* spirits."

"I think you are right, Daniel. I can't believe it! They have never given me any sort of message, much less one that says they are actually good." Noah sat down on a large rock. He seemed to be gathering his thoughts.

"Now we have nothing to worry about," Daniel joined him, relieved.

"Good job, Daniel, you understood what they were trying to tell you," Paige praised him. "It sounds like you might be right, especially since they have not bothered you since then."

"I don't want to get too comfortable. Let's stick with the plan of still being Jumbies at Carnival, since we can't be sure that the Jumbies are done with us yet," Noah said, still wanting to play it safe. "Besides, it's fun anyway."

"That's fine with me, Noah, you just need to start teaching me how to walk on these crazy stilts." They all laughed, more from relief than from humor.

"We can start right now, if you want," Noah said, "but I don't think the sand will be a good spot to learn. Let's go down town."

And off the friends went, with Paige tagging behind after gathering up her sewing materials. She did not want to miss this lesson.

30

STILT LESSONS

Walking on stilts was definitely more difficult than Daniel had thought. One false move and it was a long way to fall.

"Just remember to concentrate the whole time you are walking," Noah began to explain, "and don't look down, because it will knock you off your balance."

"Easy for you to say," Daniel said, while hobbling after his friend who was on the tallest stilts he had ever seen. "You've had a lot more practice than I've had." His steps suddenly became faster, as he lost some of his balance. He caught himself just in time.

Paige sat at a picnic table watching the escapades and continued to sew. She laughed aloud when she heard Daniel ask, "How do you get down from these things, Noah?"

"Just watch," Noah answered, as he moved toward the picnic table at full speed. Daniel watched his friend as he expertly stepped off of the stilts and onto the top of the picnic table. From there, Noah then glided safely and gracefully, landing both of his bare feet on firm ground.

Daniel followed the same path, until the bottom of his right stilt caught on a rock. Down to the hard ground he went, tumbling over his stilts. Paige ran to his rescue.

"Are you okay?" she asked, breathless.

"Yeah," Daniel said, holding the arm that he had fallen on, feeling more embarrassed than hurt. "I'm okay but I think I'm done with lessons for today."

Noah sat on the bench, leaning over and chuckling a little. "We all fall at first, Daniel. You'll get the hang of it. If your arm is okay tomorrow we'll try again. We don't have much time before Carnival and it looks like you're gonna need a lot of practice."

And practice they did. In between chores at home and sailing lessons, Noah and Daniel were able to fit in enough stilt training for Daniel to be comfortable.

One very humid June afternoon, the two friends were in the park, following one another on their stilts, when Paige slowly walked up to them, her arms full of colored material.

"I'm finally done," she said with a smile, after placing the costumes on the picnic table and wiping her brow with the back of her hand. "I hope you like them."

Daniel elegantly ambled over to the table, towering above Paige, and stepped off the stilts like an expert. "Let's see what you made. I hope the day of Carnival is not as hot as today because I'll never be able to wear all of this."

Paige giggled, and said, "Well Carnival will probably be even more unbearable and you won't be wearing all that you see here. I made one for each of us."

"You're marching in the parade too?" Daniel sounded surprised.

"Of course. You didn't think I knew how to work these things?" she said, pointing to the stilts. "I've been in every Carnival parade since I was little."

Noah joined the two of them as they held up the brightly colored costumes, talking excitedly about the upcoming event. *The best of all,* thought Daniel, *is we'll get to show the Jumbies that we can be friends.*

31

CARNIVAL DAY!

Daniel awoke on the first morning of Carnival to find his right cheek completely stuck to the sheets. "Great," was all that he could say. *This must be the hottest day yet.* He got right up out of bed anyway, with thoughts of the parade on his mind.

First, he decided to check his email. He had not heard from James in such a long time, he started to feel his old friend might have forgotten all about him.

"NO NEW MESSAGES" appeared on the computer monitor. Since there was not enough time, Daniel decided he would wait to email James again. Besides, it seemed that he was the one going to all of the trouble of trying to stay in touch. *Maybe it would help James to understand how it feels.*

Daniel was not ready to put his costume on yet, especially since his bedclothes were drenched in sweat. He shinnied down his ladder to see what was going on in the kitchen.

His mom was already awake. "Good morning, Daniel, are you ready for your big day?" She seemed to be smiling more than usual.

"I would be if we had air conditioning. Didn't Dad say he was going to get it put in soon?"

"He was, but with Grandma's cottage being built, there was not much room to breathe financially. Some day..."

"Isn't Grandma supposed to be coming today?" Daniel asked, as he opened the refrigerator door. "I don't want her to miss the best part of Carnival."

As Nancy Hawthorne wiped the sweat from her forehead, she continued to smile, and answered, "Yes, she is going to be on the 10:00 ferry if her flight is on time."

"Why are you smiling so much?" Daniel asked, with a mouthful of cereal.

"I'm just happy about Grandma coming to live here. Now we have everyone in our family in one place. Although I miss my friends." Daniel's mom glanced out the window in a daze. "I'm sure they'll come visit as soon as they hear what a paradise this island is. I'm not worried."

"I'm not either. This place is pretty cool." Daniel said, putting down his spoon for a brief moment. "I'm glad we moved here."

Nancy Hawthorne's mouth dropped, but she didn't let Daniel see her face. "You are? That means so much to me, Daniel, and your father will be happy to hear it too. I was afraid that you'd be lost without James, but it seems like you are enjoying your new friends."

"Yeah, they are nice. Besides, James is hanging out with Nick. He doesn't need me anyway." Daniel shrugged his shoulders in attempt to show his mother that he didn't care.

It did not work. "You know that isn't true, Daniel. You two have always been close friends and nothing can change that. You'll see."

"Whatever," Daniel said, thinking that his mother did not know what she was talking about. "Can you drop me by the parade on your way to the ferry? I have to fit in one last practice before I make a fool of myself in front of the whole island."

"Sure, just let me get ready," his mother said as she placed her coffee cup in the sink. "And you know that you are good at working the stilts. I've been watching you practice."

Before Daniel could ask his mom how she could have possibly seen him use the stilts, she was out of the kitchen and in her bedroom.

He walked out to the deck to try to get some air. As he slid open the glass door, a thick wave of heat slapped him across the face. *How am I ever going to wear that hot getup in the parade?* Daniel asked himself, as he quickly closed the door. He decided to bring his costume with him and put it on at the last minute.

32

A SURPRISE GUEST

When they got down to Cruz Bay, the action was already beginning. Daniel and his parents were speechless as they looked out the Jeep windows at the bright colors and happy painted faces of Carnival. Even though they had been prepared by hearing the locals discuss the event, they were still surprised by how much trouble everyone went to in order to celebrate.

As the Jeep got closer, Daniel was able to see the preparation in its entirety. There were floats made out of cars and other types of vehicles, completely decorated with many different themes.

Some had fish painted on the side, while people dressed like mermaids surrounded the float. Others were setting up a five-piece band, complete with band members dressed in long sleeves and neck ties!

Daniel looked down at his Jumbie costume, and tried to imagine putting it on.

Ben Hawthorne was talking while gazing and driving in the front seat of the Jeep. "Jonathon told me how much everyone dresses up, but this is amazing to see in person."

Pointing out the window, Daniel said, "Did you see what some people are wearing?"

"Do you mean the long sleeves?" Ben answered his son, "Those are people who have lived here their whole lives. They don't get as hot as we do."

"Oh." *That makes sense*, Daniel thought, *now I don't feel like such a heat wimp.*

"Stop, please! Can you let me out right here? I see Noah and Paige."

The Jeep came to a rolling stop. Daniel's parents both told him they'd see him soon, and to have fun. "Grandma should be here shortly," his mom said, with that familiar smile. "We'll try to bring her over before the parade starts."

Daniel barely heard the last part of his mother's comment as he stepped out of the air-conditioned Jeep, into the blazing heat.

"Noah!" he shouted, "Where are my stilts?"

Noah was already dressed, and did not seem at all bothered by the hot weather. "I laid them up against that tree. C'mon, you're late."

Daniel waved a quick hello to Paige as he dashed over to his stilts. She was putting on her purple and pink Jumbie outfit over her other clothes as she waved back. Daniel could hardly contain his excitement as he got dressed and climbed up onto his stilts.

Noah and Paige were ready to go, and Noah continued to rush Daniel. "Let's go, there is no time to practice, we have to get in the lineup."

Daniel was out of breath and already sweating in his costume. But he was determined to not let the heat bother him. Especially in front of Paige. *Why do I care?* he thought, then shook his head to himself and hurried to catch up to his island friends.

As he stood high above the crowd, Daniel combed the area for a glimpse of his grandmother, or even his parents. It also gave him a chance to see more of the brilliantly decorated floats and costumes. This was better than any parade or celebration that he had ever seen.

The people back home would never do this, Daniel thought, and then realized once again that this was his home now.

As he looked straight ahead, he saw a piece of Paige's costume catch on her stilts, and then saw her struggling to stay upright. He didn't waste any time thinking about it. He hobbled quickly over to Paige and grabbed her before she toppled over.

Paige did not even see Daniel coming. "Thank you Dan-ohhhh...noooo!"

All of a sudden, Daniel heard a loud "SNAP!" then felt the world go out from under him. The next thing he knew, he was looking up at a group of curious Jumbie faces staring down at him.

It took a long minute to discover that he was only looking at the vibrantly painted faces of people dressed up as Jumbies. "What happened?" he asked Noah.

"Your stilt snapped in half," Noah leaned down to help his friend up. "Are you okay?" he asked, with his eyebrows raised.

"I think so," Daniel brushed off his costume, which had pieces of gravel all over it. He could not manage to hide his disappointment. "I guess this means that I won't be marching in this year's Carnival."

"There's always next year," a familiar voice shouted over the crowd. Daniel snapped his head around to see who was talking to him.

"JAMES! What are you...?" Daniel was speechless. He looked up to see his mother, beaming, then glanced quickly back at James. He could hardly believe his eyes as he hobbled over to James, and gave him a friendly tap on the arm.

James was laughing. "I can't believe we pulled off this surprise. I didn't want to email you since I wanted you to think that I'd forgotten about our plans to meet here."

Daniel tried to catch his breath and gather his thoughts, all at the same time. It suddenly occurred to him that the official Carnival parade had already started.

He looked up just in time to see Paige waving to him, with Noah not far behind. *They knew about this the whole time,* he thought.

"Who are they?" James asked, as he began to take in the island surroundings.

"They're just some friends," Daniel said, while gently rubbing his leg. "You'll like them."

"What about the girl?"

"That's just Paige, she's just a friend too," Daniel said as he turned his usual shade of pink.

James knew the signs. "Whatever you say..."

In all of the excitement, Daniel had almost forgotten about his dear Grandma.

"I'm right here, Sweetie," she said, on cue, as she opened her arms to greet her grandson. "I hope you are surprised. We had quite a time trying to bring this one here without you knowing," she said, pointing to James.

"You were in on this too?" Daniel was still shocked.

"Of course. How do you think he got here? Now let's watch this crazy Carnival that you all have been telling me about. I might as well get used to it since this is my new home." She left to join Daniel's parents.

Daniel looked over at James, finally absorbing the fact that he had come all this way just to see him. "So, what do you think?" he asked.

"Not bad," James answered.

That reminded Daniel about something. "I will have to fill you in on everything."

"Yeah. And I want to see a real Jumbie," James said.

Daniel looked back up at the parade, while mentally checking his most recent injuries, then turned back to James. "Can you hang on a minute?"

"Sure," said James, looking slightly confused. "What are you going to do?"

"Show you a real Jumbie," said Daniel with a big smile.

A few minutes later, Daniel was once again high up over the crowd, walking carefully on the stilts that he had lashed together with some material from his costume. It took a simple, quick-minded rigging, and maybe a little healing magic from the Jumbies.

On that day, as Daniel stood proudly in half of his Jumbie costume in the Caribbean heat, he was happier than he had ever been. And he finally came to realize what he thought Jumbies were all about.

He marched proudly over to his good friend James, who came so far to see him, and said, "You know what, James? The Jumbies are scary but maybe they aren't so bad, after all."

James stood up on his tip toes and gave Daniel a high five. "Maybe you are right, Daniel." Then he smiled brightly, and continued, "Now let's talk about how I can get a pair of those stilts for next year's Carnival…"

THE END…
(But more of Daniel's Adventures on Island Soon Come!)

ABOUT THE AUTHOR

Jules has been writing and imagining since she was a young girl. The joy of her life is her family, as well as the extraordinary friends who also light up her world. Jules lives at the beach in sunny Florida with her sweet hubby and precious son, and is about due for another trip to the magically beautiful tropical island of St. John…

28338228R00076

Made in the USA
Charleston, SC
09 April 2014